SUPER BADDIES

Baddies vs. Goodies

WRITTEN BY
M.C. BADGER

ILLUSTRATED & DESIGNED BY
SIMON SWINGLER

That's right – my family lives in a volcano. Today's the first day of term at Baddie Primary, and I can't wait to go back!

Our volcano erupts at the same time every day, so I always use the extra boost to get me all the way to the bus stop.

4

5

I couldn't wait to show my baddie buds all the stunts I'd been working on.

I call this one the *Trail Blazer*.

This one's the *Ring of Fire!*

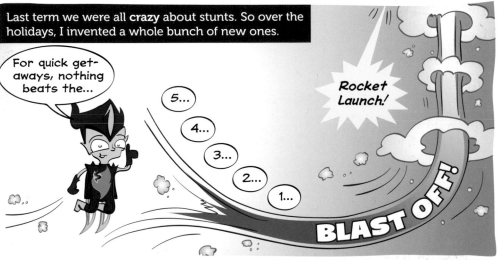

Last term we were all **crazy** about stunts. So over the holidays, I invented a whole bunch of new ones.

For quick get-aways, nothing beats the...

5...
4...
3...
2...
1...

Rocket Launch!

BLAST OFF!

Baddies love stunts, because they're cool, fun and dangerous. And goodies hate them for the same reason! This makes stunts perfect for goodie-annoying.

There's the bus stop!

FOOOM!

BADDIE P.S.

GOODIE P.S.

9

THE
PER
DIES
I'm Scorcher and I can make fire. I'm pretty hot stuff!
I'm Frosty and I can make ice out of thin air. Cool, huh?
Well, I'm Mean Streak and I'm super speedy!

Now that introductions were out of the way, I wanted to know what my friends had done over the holidays.

So, did you guys invent any new stunts over the summer? Because I –

ZIP!

Nope.

Me neither.

We've been inventing gadgets instead!

Oh?

Gadgets are the coolest, Scorcher! Here's my latest invention – the *Instant Beach.*

It makes a *huge* sandy mess.

Wow!

INSTANT BEACH

And I invented these *Crusher Gloves.*

For *destroying* stuff!

13

BADDIE P.S.

Go Meanie, go!

SIGN BENT LAST TERM IN EXPLOSION

BADDIE P.S.

SUCKER! PPPP-p! PPPPP-p!

Whoa! That's totally bad.

Thanks! I call them *Speedy Grippers* because they can climb anything!

Want to see me run up a tree?

You bet!

My buddies' gadgets were awesome.

And Meanie was pretty bad too!

Go baddies, go!

WHOOZZZZ!

BADDIE P.S.

GOODIE P.S.

14

Of course, it didn't take long for the goodies to spoil our fun.

Hey! You stepped on our side of the bus stop!

SCREECH!

IT'S JUST OVER!

They're always **so** uptight.

Seriously, does it matter?

Of course it matters! You're a *baddie* now. You better not do it again.

And that's why we **love** to mess with them.

Hang on, *where's* the dividing line?

Right there.

Oh, here.

Yes. There.

Especially when they make it so easy for us.

OK goodies, I promise I won't *walk* on your side.

Ha-ha-ha!

Tee-hee-hee!

Gasp!

Oh no! This yellow, dust-like substance is everywhere!

Our bus stop is ruined! *Ruined!*

Sheesh! It's just *sand.*

It won't *hurt* you.

Won't *hurt* us? It almost got in our *eyes!*

And our under-pants!

I'm calling the emergency crew.

Itch-itch!

That's the problem with goodies. Everything has to turn into a huge battle!

Our bus was late as usual, but that didn't matter – baddies are almost never on time. We were just happy to be back at Baddie Primary!

It's the greatest school in the world. Some of the baddest baddies **ever** went here.

TREMMA
Invented trampoline footpaths.

FIBBERSKI
Created a dishonesty serum to help you fib.

Here at last!

DRASTICO
Tried to turn every day into Saturday.

19

Now that we were level-three baddies, we were going to learn some really cool stuff— like Evil Cackling and Big Explosions.

Hey – does anyone know who our teacher is this year?

Level Three

I just hope it's not that *suddenly appearing* guy...

Greetings, my little badlings!

Dr Thunder!

APPEAR!

Oh, great!

Dr Thunder was such a dweeb.

Oh yes, it is I! The very same *Dr Thunder* who created the infamous *evil* chocolate-fountain factory!

And just like that, the term had begun.

Now, today we're going to write about what *kind* of baddie you want to be when you grow up.

Any ideas?

A baddie stunt guy!

A *mad* scientist!!

A henchman!

Excellent, badlings! Let's get writing.

Lad, you look like a bright spark.

Hand out these work-books and try not to burn them, OK?

As soon as I saw the workbooks, I knew something was wrong.

Baddie Workbook. Level 3

These don't look like *baddie* workbooks. They're too neat.

Flaming fireballs!

Stand back, everyone. These books have been *goodified!*

How to keep your bus stop **CLEAN**

How to keep **SAND** out of your undies

It's the goodies' revenge!

Gasp!

SNEAKY GOODIE

GOODNESS RAY

It was **sneaky**. But it was also the perfect chance to use one of my stunts. I could burn those books to a crisp in mid-air!

I wasn't about to let the goodies get away with their **revenge**. They'd completely over-reacted! If those dorks wanted a battle, they would **get** a battle.

I didn't need to watch out for the goodies. I had the baddies on my side!

As we headed for the storeroom, the playground was quiet. **Too** quiet.

Those goodies are so lousy. The bus-stop thing was just a joke!

Tell me about it. They take *boring* to a whole new level!

Yeah.

Grinades are the worst. If they get too close to your face, you'll be stuck with a big dumb smile for a **week**.

CHEESE!

Erk!

Too late! What do we do now?

Luckily, Bad Mads had a gadget ready.

Quick! Use my *Stink Bombs*. They'll wipe the smile off anyone's face.

STINK BOMB

One for us, and two for you!

Ahhh!

Not stink bombs!

DROP!

But the goodies were prepared too.

Quick! Put these on!

ANTI-STINK MASKS

WHIP!

29

The Cool Ray froze the speakers and...

...made the music cool!

We were sure we'd finally beaten them!

Then something struck me. (Luckily, it wasn't a carrot.)

Hang on...

Save yourselves!

If these were **heat-seeking** Dyno-Carrots, and I was the **hottest** baddie around...

What are you doing?

WHOOSH!

Watch and learn, my friend!

Then my stunts were the perfect way to save the day.

First up, the *Trail Blazer!*

BLAAM!

WHIRRRR....

Then, the *Ring of Fire!*

WHIRRRR....

40

Are you a baddie or a goodie?

Just answer the questions and follow the arrows to find out!

Start here!

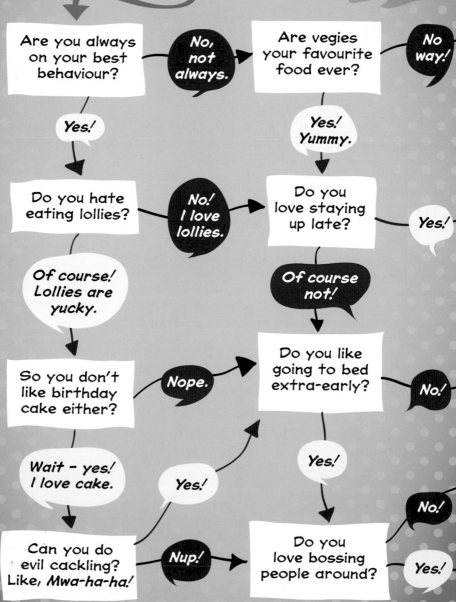

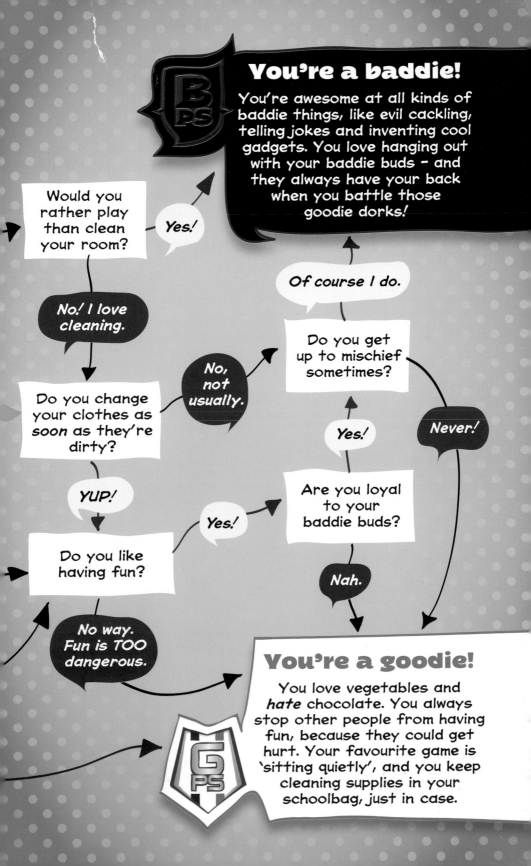

Have you read all the SUPER BADDIES books?

Baddies vs. Goodies

M.C. BADGER & SIMON SWINGLER

When Robots Go Bad

M.C. BADGER & SIMON SWINGLER

Bad News Birthday

M.C. BADGER & SIMON SWINGLER

Running Riot

M.C. BADGER & SIMON SWINGLER

Bad News Birthday and *Running Riot* are coming soon to all *bad* bookstores!

Meet the REAL baddies behind the SUPER BADDIES.

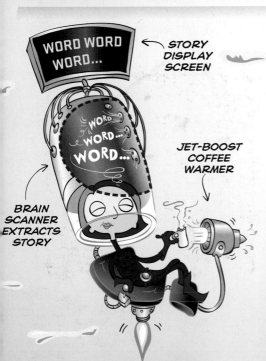

WORD WORD WORD...

← STORY DISPLAY SCREEN

WORD WORD... WORD...

JET-BOOST COFFEE WARMER

BRAIN SCANNER EXTRACTS STORY

AUTHOR

CODE NAME:
M.C. Badger

To most people, M. C. Badger appears to be a normal person living with her family in Germany. Only a few know her true identity: The Imaginator. Under the cover of night, The Imaginator zips around the world on her trusty coffee-powered Story-Jet 5000, whipping up evil plots from thin air!

ILLUSTRATOR

CODE NAME:
Simon Swingler

Simon Swingler is an evil genius who invented the baddest gadget ever: the **Illustron**. There's only one prototype in the whole world and Simon uses it to draw the Super Baddies books. Simon and his family now guard the **Illustron** from a secret location in Australia. Like all awesome baddies, Simon's favourite food is chocolate.

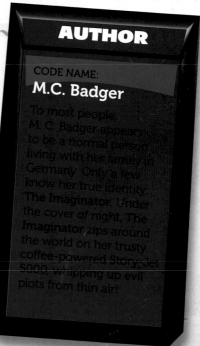

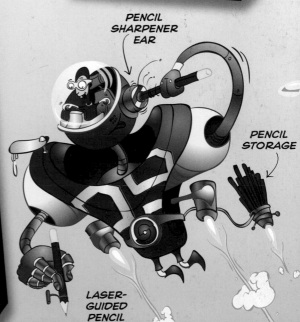

PENCIL SHARPENER EAR

PENCIL STORAGE

LASER-GUIDED PENCIL